About the Author

Shabana is a designer who loves to write and illustrate. She is inspired by other cultures around the world and loves to observe trends and design changes in everyday life for inspiration. Her fuel is a secret blend of tea and malted milk biscuits.

Shabana Ahmed

ONION BUDDY

AUSTIN MACAULEY PUBLISHERS™

LONDON * CAMBRIDGE * NEW YORK * SHARJAH

A CIP catalogue record for this title is available from the British Library.

ISBN 9781528904261 (Paperback)
ISBN 9781528904278 (Hardback)
ISBN 9781528904285 (E-Book)

www.austinmacauley.com

First Published (2018)
Austin Macauley Publishers™ Ltd
25 Canada Square
Canary Wharf
London
E14 5LQ

Dedication

For Amoo and Papa, the best storytellers and optimists I have ever known.

Acknowledgements

A special thanks to my sister, Yasmin, for being so encouraging in the journey of *Onion Buddy*.

Little Onion buddy was the last son of a well-known root. He was not as big as his three brothers. They were all round and shiny, with impressive skin stripes, and looked great in their posh sunglasses on a sunny day. You see, Onion buddy was a pop dash smaller, he hadn't grown into his stripes yet, and too much sun hurt his eyes.

Did I mention that he wasn't the most popular kid at school? On sports day, he ran for his life and did rather well at the one hundred metre sprint, beating Tomato Girl, Aubergine Boy and the Twin Peas. But it was a shame that his sweat made everyone's eyes sting. He had to wear a paper bag on the winner's podium, so the runners-up didn't cry at the award ceremony.

Sometimes, there were days where life was a bit hard for Onion buddy, he wished he was like everyone else. Getting picked for sports teams was tricky, and no matter how much milk he drank with his dinner, he was still shorter and smaller than his big brothers.

But Onion buddy had the best mum in Vegetable Patch Village. She always told him that the best was yet to come and when it did, he would be just amazing. She would also make him special hot chocolate and buttered crumpets on rainy dinner days and told him many stories about his lively grandparents, who he never had the chance to meet.

These stories, along with his mum's positivity, gave him little bags of strength, and he would remember her words on the days that were gloomy and boo hoo.

Something happened when Onion buddy turned seven. It was marvellous and new. His hair started growing and growing....and growing until he had long bright-green wonderful lengths of the most eye-catching hair.

Unfortunately, the kids at school didn't think it was wonderful though. They giggled in class behind his back and made fun of him in the canteen, saying that he looked like a green haired alien from Mars eating peanut butter sandwiches!

For a while, Onion buddy did his best to control his hair. He cut it twice a week, but it just grew back so quickly and sometimes even greener than before!

He wore a fisherman's hat to school, but the teacher confiscated it. He didn't like the name calling and started to feel sad inside. It made him feel blue and left out of everything.

After some time, he finally realised that no matter how hard he tried, he couldn't change himself or hide his hair anymore, so Onion buddy decided to make things better. He made a decision to be the best version of himself.

WELCOME TO
HARVEST PRIMARY
SCHOOL

He was so excited about feeling brave and strong that he told himself he was going to be amazing every day, no matter what happened. It started with a bubble bath. A lovely hot bubbly soak in the tub. He polished his skin with soap until he was shiny again; then lay in the tub and thought about all the new and fun things he was fully determined to be and do.

Then he chose one of the brother's fancy shampoos and massaged a glorious lather into his dull green hair. He covered his whole head in bubbles and breathed in the sweet-smelling shampoo and smiled to himself.

Onion buddy dried his hair and looked in the mirror. He made a promise to take care of his long bright-green eye-catching hair, combing it carefully and taking in the glorious colours he had never noticed before.

The following day, Onion buddy was a different boy at school. He walked into the classroom with his head held high and was looking very confident. All the kids were surprised to see him like this, he looked fantastic and free. His hair was perfectly combed up into a high quiff and was catching the light of the sun when he spoke.

HARVEST PRIMARY SCHOOL

The next day he continued being the best version of himself, he couldn't help it, he was going to stay strong and feel as wonderful as can be!
Every day, Onion buddy's hair changed; sometimes he popped it into a bow or wore it down, and other times he let it do anything it liked! Nothing or no one

would stop him now, he finally loved his long bright-green eye-catching hair and was proud to be who he was. Mum was right, the best was yet to come and it did, and he was just amazing after all.